THE FOUR FRANKS

To my son Frank and my dad
who sailed the sea in ships
S.M.

To Katie
G.P.

First published in Great Britain 2003
by Egmont Books Ltd
239 Kensington High Street, London W8 6SA
Text copyright © Sue Mayfield 2003
Illustrations copyright © Garry Parsons 2003
The author and illustrator have asserted their moral rights
Paperback ISBN 1 4052 0674 8
10 9 8 7 6 5 4 3 2 1
A CIP catalogue record for this title is available from the British Library
Printed in U.A.E.

THE FOUR FRANKS

Sue Mayfield · Garry Parsons

Go Bananas

Hello, I'm Frank
– Frank the fourth,
in fact!
I'm named after my
dad, Frank the third.
Dad is named after
his dad, my grandpa,
Frank the second.
And Grandpa is
named after his dad,
my great-grandpa,
Frank the first.
So that's us . . .
the four Franks!

My name's Frank.

I'm Frank as well.

Me too.

And me!

And then there's Franco. He's
Great-grandpa Frank's parrot. He
talks all the time, mainly in Spanish.

They met years ago, long before
I was born. Long before Dad was
born. Even before Grandpa was born.

Franco is almost as old as
Great-grandpa Frank . . . and
that's VERY OLD!

Great-grandpa is so old, he's practically an antique! He is ninety-eight years old. That's nearly a hundred!

Grandpa is sixty-six years old. Dad is thirty-eight years old. And I was six last week.

For my birthday, Dad, Grandpa
and Great-grandpa Frank gave me
a fantastic present. It was a sailing
ship, yellow and black with three
masts and white sails. 'It's beautiful,'
I said.

'It's just like the one I sailed in,'
said Great-grandpa Frank.

Great-grandpa Frank was a sailor
long ago.

Once he was in a terrible storm.

Great-grandpa Frank had to cling
on to the mast of his ship to keep
from being thrown overboard.

During the storm, the ship ran

aground on some rocks.

When the storm died down, it was

stuck there. Great-grandpa Frank

had to swim to the shore!

I couldn't wait to sail my boat.

Tucking it under my arm, I ran

across the field behind my house to

the stream. It's only a little stream,

but it had been raining and the water

was swirly and strong.

I put the model ship into the stream
by the bridge. It sailed fast, speeding
through the water like a swan. A
breeze blew against the sails and
made them flutter like flags.

I ran along the bank watching my
boat sail by.

But then the ship began to travel faster

and faster – faster than I could run.

It bobbed and twirled in the current.

Soon my ship was out of reach.

'Help!' I shouted. But the ship rushed

on, tossed by the gurgling stream.

'Stop!' I yelled. But it was no good.

In a moment, the ship was gone.

The last I saw of it was a flash of

white, disappearing down into a pipe.

I had lost the special ship.

I remembered their faces when

I unwrapped it. It didn't feel like

a happy birthday now.

I was so ashamed that I ran home

and hid in my room. I didn't say

a word to anyone.

But later on, at teatime, everyone was talking about the model ship.

'Where's your ship, Frank?' said Dad.

'It's in my room,' I lied. I felt my face go red.

'Great-grandpa Frank made that ship for me on my sixth birthday,' said Grandpa.

'That was during World War II,' said Great-grandpa Frank. 'I carved the ship from a block of wood. I made the masts from knitting needles, and the sails from cotton flour bags.' Great-grandpa smiled to himself as he remembered.

Then Grandpa said, 'In the war, when I was your age, children were sent away from the cities to live in the countryside where it was safer.

No bombs, you see.

I went away, on a train, all by myself,

to stay with a kind family on a farm.

I took the model ship with me and when I was homesick, I used to sail it on the duck pond.

One day, I tore the ship's sail on a thorny bush, and the farmer's wife mended it with a needle and thread. You can still see the mend,' he said. 'I'll show you after tea.'

I gulped.

Then it was Dad's turn to tell a story

about the model ship.

'Grandpa gave

the ship to me

when I was

little,' he said.

'I used to sail it on

the lake in the park,' said Dad.

'Where that skateboard park is

now,' said Grandpa.

'One day,' Dad said, 'the ship

crashed into a rowing boat and one

of the masts snapped in two.'

'I mended it with chopsticks from

the new Chinese restaurant on the

corner!' said Grandpa with a chuckle.

'You mended it the day the first person landed on the moon,' said Dad. 'I remember we were watching on TV.'

'So we were,' said Grandpa.

'And now it's your ship, Frank,' said Great-grandpa Frank. 'It's belonged to all of us, that

ship has,' said Grandpa. 'It's the four

Franks' ship in fact.' Everybody laughed. Everybody except me, that is.

That night I couldn't sleep.

I thought of
Great-grandpa
Frank carefully
carving the
boat.

I thought of
Grandpa
going away
on the train.

I thought of Dad, playing in the park and the man on the moon.

It was our ship – the four Franks' ship. And I had lost it. How could I ever bring myself to tell them?

The next day, we went for a walk.

All four of us, the four Franks.

We went along the promenade,

beside the sea.

'What's up, Frank?' asked Dad.

'You seem a bit gloomy,'

said Grandpa.

'I'm fine,' I said. But I wasn't. I was worrying about the lost ship.

We stopped to look at the sea. Dad bought ice creams. 'Shall we go down on the beach?' he said.

Part way along the shore there were
some rocks covered in seaweed. A
little stream cut on to the beach, and
made a swervy pattern in the sand.
I took off my socks and shoes so
I could paddle in the stream.

Then an amazing thing happened.

Dad saw it first. 'That looks like . . .

No! It can't be . . .' He pointed to

the rocks.

There on the rocks was something small, something black and yellow and white. I ran closer. My heart was pounding. It couldn't be. But it was. IT WAS! It was the ship. It was the four Franks' model ship!

The stream must have carried it
right on to the beach, and it had
run aground on some rocks, just
like Great-grandpa Frank's ship
in the storm.

I bent down and lifted the ship off
the rocks. It was a bit battered.
Some of the rigging had snapped,
a sail was torn and the paint was
rather scratched.

I was so relieved to see it that I burst
into tears. Everybody stared at me.

'I lost it!' I cried. 'I lost it in the stream yesterday, but I was too ashamed to tell you. I'm sorry!' Dad hugged me and gave me his hanky.

'It will mend,'
said Great-
grandpa
Frank.

'It will soon be
as good as new,'
said Grandpa.

'And one day, you can give it to your children,' said Dad squeezing my arm, 'and I wonder where they'll play with it . . . ?'

We mended it together. Great-grandpa Frank told us what to do.

Grandpa tied the knots in the rigging.

Dad stitched the sail.

There. Nearly finished!

And I painted it.

Just one more coat of paint.

'I think we should give the ship a new name,' said Great-grandpa Frank when we had finished. 'We'll call her *The Four Franks*. Long may she sail!' And we all cheered.

And before that it belonged to his grandpa.

His great-grandpa Frank made the ship from wood.

I used cotton flour bags to make the sails.

Think about your favourite toy.
What is it made of? Is it new or old?
What makes it your favourite?
Can you draw a picture or make
a list of your favourite toys?

Guess the Toy

'The Four Franks' is Frank's favourite toy now, but it hasn't always been – he's played with lots of different things. Can you work out which toys Frank used to play with when he was younger?

Aged 3 months

Aged 1 year

Aged 2 years

Aged 3 years

Aged 4 years

Aged 5 years

Aged 6 years

Toys from the past

How do you think you can find out about toys from the past? Why not ask your mum or dad or grandparents to tell you about the toys they played with when they were small.

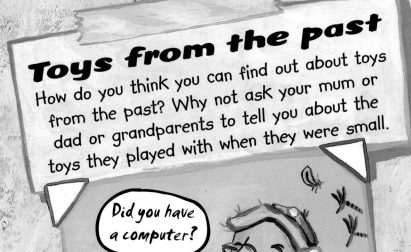

Here's what Frank's family said . . .

Grandpa

I loved to play with my train set. I wanted to be an engine driver – all aboard!

Great-grandpa

I used to love my teddy bear. I still have him, but he's very old now. Nearly as old as I am!

Mix and Match

Can you match the words to the toys?

Soft   Broken   Wooden   Rusty   Plastic   Noisy